Have You Ever Seen an Elephant Sneeze?

Have You Ever Seen an Elephant Sneeze?

A Zany Zooful of God's Creatures

Bernadette McCarver Snyder

Illustrations by Jim Richter

AVE MARIA PRESS Notre Dame, Indiana 46556

Dedication

I dedicate this book to William Daniel Snyder, otherwise known as Will, otherwise known as bright-eyed, busy and full of questions. I hope he will enjoy the discoveries in this zany zoo as much as I enjoy watching him discover the zany and wonder-filled world God made for him to explore!

© 1996 by Ave Maria Press, Inc., Notre Dame, IN 46556

International Standard Book Number: 0-87793-589-0

Library of Congress Catalog Card Number   96-85250

Cover and text design by Elizabeth J. French

Cover and text illustrations by Jim Richter

Printed and bound in the United States of America.

Contents

Introduction

God Made WHAT?

When God made the world, he must have had a lot of fun. He could make whatever kind of animal, vegetable or mineral that he wanted. He could put into the world whatever colors or shapes or designs suited his fancy. And God IS very fancy—making all the strange and wonderful things we find today on this planet earth.

But what if YOU could have made the world?

Would YOU have made things the same way God did? OR—would you have made the sky purple instead of blue and lions green instead of gold? Would you have made onions taste like chocolate or chocolate taste like green beans?

Whatever kind of world you made, it would have been very hard to make one more exciting or surprising than the world God made.

Let's take a look at just a few of the strange and amazing animals God made and put in the world for YOU to discover!

Who Knows Whose Nose This Is?

This nose has 100,000 muscles. Now that's a lot of muscle! And this nose has a funny name—a name that sounds like the back of an automobile. Yep, you guessed right. It's a trunk—an elephant's trunk!

God put 100,000 muscles into an elephant's trunk-nose so it would be nimble enough to pick up a single blade of grass—but strong enough to knock down a great big tree!

The elephant NEEDS a nose like that because sometimes he wants to eat a tiny blade of grass. Other times he works as a hired helper to make a clearing in the jungle by knocking down big trees.

YOUR nose doesn't have 100,000 muscles because God knew you wouldn't want to pick up grass or knock down trees with your nose!

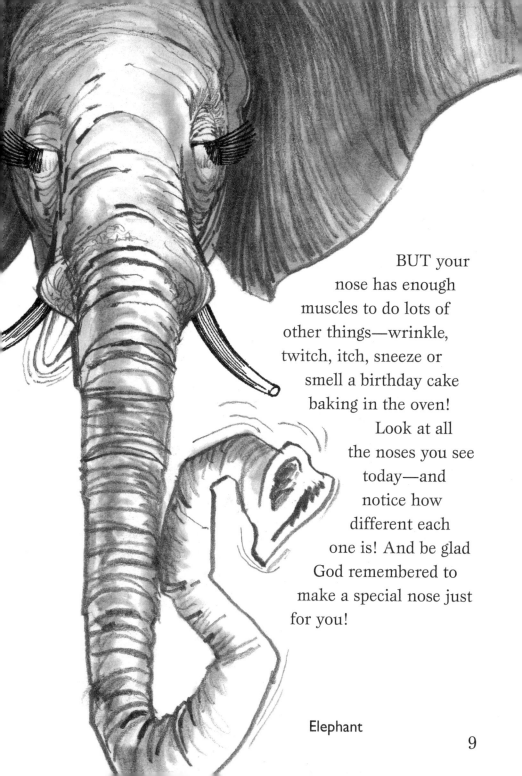

BUT your nose has enough muscles to do lots of other things—wrinkle, twitch, itch, sneeze or smell a birthday cake baking in the oven! Look at all the noses you see today—and notice how different each one is! And be glad God remembered to make a special nose just for you!

Elephant

9

The Speedy Cat: Faster Than a Speeding Locomotive

Out in the jungle, there's a cat—not a cat in a hat or on a mat or holding a bat—but a very FAST cat. This cat is called a cheetah and for short sprints, she can run 60 miles an hour. That's faster than an Olympic medal winner could run. That's faster than some locomotives can barrel down the tracks! That's faster than the speed limit on some highways!

Have you ever seen a cat that can run that fast? Have you ever owned a cat that can run that fast? Can YOU run that fast?

Well, of course you can't. God didn't make your legs work like a cheetah's legs work because you don't live out in the jungle. You don't NEED to run as fast as 60 miles an hour.

But sometimes you DO need to run pretty fast—to do an errand or run in a race or play a game. If you have to run fast today, tell God thanks for legs and muscles and crazy cats like cheetahs who can run faster than some highway speed limits!

Cheetah

Why Does That Frog Have a Parachute?

Asian Tree Frog

Did you ever see a frog by a pond or lake or maybe in your back yard? Did any of those frogs have parachutes?

Well, the Asian tree frog "flies" like people do with parachutes! God made this frog with very long toes—and in between each toe is a fold of skin like the webs on a duck's feet. These frogs live in trees. When they want to move to a different tree, they leap into the air and their webbed feet fill with air just like a parachute and they float down to the next tree!

You don't have parachute toes because you don't need to move from tree to tree. When you need to move around, you can walk or crawl or jump or run—or maybe use a bike or roller blades. Frogs don't have bikes or roller blades, but Asian tree frogs DO have parachutes!

Pretend today that you are a tree frog, flying from tree to tree with your parachute. Close your eyes and imagine what the tree frog might see as he flies through the jungle. Do you see a bird, a snake, a leaf, a rock, a monkey, or another tree frog?

Isn't it fun to pretend? Aren't you glad God gave you an imagination instead of a parachute?

What Big Ears YOu HaVe!

Fennec

In the desert, there are a lot of unusual animals. One of them is a desert fox. The very SMALLEST desert fox is only 18 inches long—about as long as a loaf of French bread. But its ears are four inches long. Now that doesn't sound so long until you think about the fact that its ears are almost one-fourth as long as it is tall. That would be like a six-foot tall man having ears as long as that loaf of French bread!

Can you imagine how that man would look? Can you imagine how YOU would look if your ears were one-fourth as long as you are tall?

The small desert fox with the long ears is called a fennec and lives in the Sahara desert, but the little kit foxes who live in the American southwest also have very large ears. God made their ears that way so they could hear the softest

sounds in the dark when they are out in the desert at night looking for food.

Aren't you glad you don't have to go out in the desert at night to look for food? Aren't you glad you have ears to hear when someone calls to tell you lunch is ready?

Use your ears today to listen to all the small sounds around you. How many different small sounds can you hear with those wonderful SMALL ears God gave you?

Clean as a Pig?

Would you like to take a nap in a mud puddle? Probably not. But pigs do! Why? Because they have very sensitive skin. Yes, they do!

Rolling—or napping—in a cool mud puddle protects a pig's skin from insects that bite and sun that burns. But just because a pig rolls around in the mud, don't think he LIKES being dirty. Actually, a pig is naturally a very clean animal who would prefer to cool off in some nice clean water. But a pig don't usually have his own swimming pool, so he has to do the best he can with what he's got. If he lives on a farm, that usually means a mud puddle!

Of course, ALL pigs don't live on farms. Some live in the city. Some pigs are even Secret Agents! That's right! Pigs are very intelligent and can be trained just like dogs—so some

pigs have been trained to work with police and sniff out drugs! Have you ever seen a Secret Agent pig in a police officer's car? Have you ever rolled around in a mud puddle? Have you ever acted piggish?

Some people would whine and complain if they only had a cool mud puddle instead of a fancy swimming pool. But God made pigs smart enough to do the best they can with what they've got. Are YOU as smart as a pig?

Pig

A Bashful "Knight" in Shining Armor

Did you ever hear stories about knights who wore clothes made out of steel? Those shiny metal suits were called "armor" and they protected the brave soldiers who rode out to fight battles using only swords and spears.

Armadillo

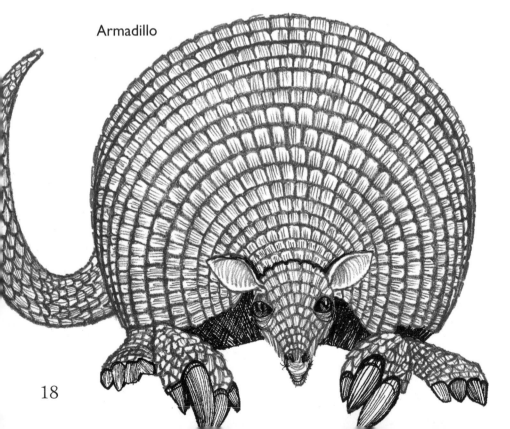

Did you know God made an animal with a bony covering that LOOKS like a suit of armor? And it has a name that sounds like its suit! This animal is called an armadillo. A strange thing about the armadillo is that it wears armor to protect itself from enemies, but it is really bashful and doesn't like to fight! And it has very soft teeth—so it always eats soft food (no crunchy chips, cookies or corn on the cob!)

Instead of strong teeth, God gave the armadillo long, strong claws and powerful arms so it can dig faster than a dog! The armadillo can dig through leaves to find soft bugs for dinner but it can also dig a hole VERY fast so it can climb in and hide from an enemy—when it doesn't want to use that armor!

Would YOU like to have a suit of armor? That would be fun IF you could take it OFF sometimes. The armadillo needs that armor ALL the time but you don't—so that's probably why God gave you a suit of skin instead!

Have you ever really looked at your skin? Or thought about what a nice "container" it is for your bony skeleton? Put your hand in a bowl of warm water today and leave it there until it gets all wrinkled. Then take it out and watch the wrinkles go away. Isn't it nice to have a soft, changeable, flexible skin suit instead of one of armor?

The No-Sweat, Swimming, Dreaming Dog

Did you know that dogs never have to take swimming lessons? God "programmed" them so that when they are born, they already know how to swim! A one-month old baby does NOT know how to swim but a puppy does. If you take a teeny tiny puppy that is only one month old and hold it over a tub of water, it will automatically start to move its legs in a swimming motion—the way YOU would move to swim the "dog paddle"!

And did you know a dog never perspires like people do? It's true—no sweat! When you get hot—when you run or play ball on a summer day—your body cools itself off by making you perspire. But when dogs get overheated, they cool off by panting. Did you ever see a dog with her mouth open and her tongue hanging out, panting? She's trying to cool herself off—or maybe she's trying to tell you she needs a drink of water!

And did you ever see a dog dreaming? Some scientists think that when a dog whines or wags its tail while it's asleep, it may be dreaming!

Do
YOU ever
swim, sweat
or dream? Sure
you do! You might
even do the "dog paddle" in the
swimming pool, pant when you are
hot or dream about puppy
dogs! Whatever you do
today or ANY day,
remember that God
"programmed" YOU to
be good, be kind, be
honest—and be
happy. So always
try to BE your
doggone best!
That's the way to
have a GOOD
day, no sweat!

Dog

21

How Many Logs Would a Woodchuck Saw If a Woodchuck Could Saw Logs?

When your grandpa gets tired, he might tell you it's time for him to go "saw logs." That's a funny expression people sometimes use to say they're going to take a nap or go to sleep. Well, a woodchuck saws logs a lot!

Before winter comes, the woodchuck eats plenty of plants, roots and bark in

Woodchuck

order to store up fat in its body. Then when the weather gets cold and the woodchuck can't find any more food, he digs a deep "burrow" or underground tunnel. The woodchuck crawls into the burrow and hibernates. He goes to sleep and sleeps through the whole cold winter!

The word "hibernate" means "winter sleep" but it is not ordinary sleep—the way YOU sleep when you go to bed at night. The woodchuck (like other animals who hibernate) breathes VERRRY slowly so he doesn't need much oxygen and his body VERRRY slowly burns up the fat for fuel so he doesn't need extra food.

When spring comes and the earth gets warm, the woodchuck wakes up and crawls out of the tunnel. And boy, is he hungry! He eats and eats. Wouldn't you?

The next time you get tired and sleepy and feel like "sawing logs," don't forget to say your goodnight prayers. Ask God to bless you and your family and woodchucks and woodpeckers and wood-cutters and sleepy grandpas. And maybe you'll want to tell God thank you for letting you sleep in a warm, cozy bed instead of an underground tunnel!

Watch Your Tongue!

Cat

Do you know what animal has a tongue that can be used as a washcloth, hairbrush, knife, and fork? That's right. It's the kitty cat.

Have you ever watched a cat take a bath? Instead of using a washcloth, she uses her tongue! She cleans herself all up by licking every single spot—until she gets to her neck and head. The tongue can't reach there but that doesn't stop the kitty cat. She licks her paw and uses that to clean the spots her tongue can't reach. And then she smoothes down her hair with the tongue, just like you might use a hairbrush.

When it's time for dinner, the kitty uses her tongue to lap up milk or food just like you might use a knife and fork. So the kitty cat doesn't need a washcloth, hairbrush, knife or fork—because God gave her a very special tongue!

God gave YOU a special tongue too—but not to use to take a bath or brush your hair. God gave you a tongue to lick stamps and lollipops, to say hello and shout hooray, to sing and to pray. How will you use your tongue today? Will you say mean things and hurt someone? Will you say funny things and make someone laugh? Be careful which words you let fall out of your mouth! And tonight at dinner when you use your knife and lick your fork, tell God thanks for your tongue—and be glad you don't have to use it to wash behind your ears!

Making Tracks!

Mr. Lion spends a lot of time "lion" around! Although the male lion is known as the King of the Jungle, he sleeps about 18 hours a day. Female lions are left to take care of the cubs and even do some of the hunting. But, if Mr. Lion would just stand up straight, he could be a great basketball player! You know why? A grown-up male lion is about nine feet long. If he could stand up on his hind legs instead of walking on all fours like he does, he would be taller than today's tallest basketball star!

And he has big feet too. When people on a safari are tracking a lion, they can always tell if it is a lady or a gentleman lion because Mr. Lion has the bigger front paws.

Why don't you do some tracking yourself today? If the weather is warm enough, ask your friends or family to get their bare feet wet and then "make tracks" on a concrete sidewalk or driveway. See who has the biggest feet, the

Lion

widest feet, the longest toes. Get out your watch and check the time to see how long it takes the tracks to dry. And think about how God made your feet different from the lion's paws.

The shape, the bones, the muscles, even the toenails are different—and God designed them that way so you can do things the lion can't. You can tiptoe, dance, scrunch up your toes, stand up straight and play basketball! Even if you're not nine feet tall!

It's a Stretch– But the View Is Great!

Why do you guess God gave the giraffe such a LOOOOONG neck? Well, for one thing, the giraffe is so tall, she can see for miles around. If an enemy (like a lion or a hunter) is coming, the giraffe can get away in a hurry.

And there's another good reason. The giraffe can reach leaves the other animals can't—on the very tip-top of the trees. And giraffes love leaves, especially the leaves of the acacia tree.

28

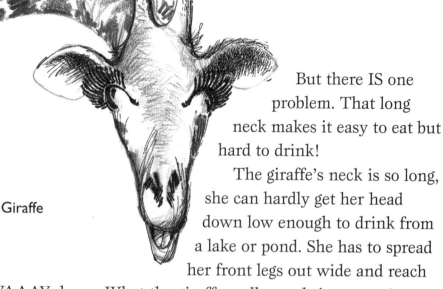

Giraffe

But there IS one problem. That long neck makes it easy to eat but hard to drink!

The giraffe's neck is so long, she can hardly get her head down low enough to drink from a lake or pond. She has to spread her front legs out wide and reach WAAAY down. What the giraffe really needs is a straw!

Aren't you glad you have a regular-size neck so you can get a drink from a water fountain? Aren't you glad restaurants have straws so you can sip a cool cola or a chocolate shake?

While you're thinking about this tall giraffe today, why don't you get out a ruler and measure to see how long YOUR neck is? How long is your arm, your leg, your little finger? Maybe you could measure yourself in pennies! Start today to collect pennies. When you have a lot, place them in a straight line on the floor. Lay next to the line and count to see how many pennies you are long. Are you worth $10, $15, $20? To God, you're worth more than ANY amount of money! God made you. God loves you.

Just the way you are.

The Caped Crusader

Have you noticed that Superman and other "super heroes" wear capes? One such hero is even called "The Caped Crusader" because he wears a cape and is always around when somebody needs help. This animal doesn't really wear a cape but he DOES have a lot of fur around his shoulders that LOOKS like a cape. And you know what? There was a time when he was "always around" when somebody needed a nickel!

This big brown shaggy animal is called a buffalo, or bison—and a long time ago, there were 50 million buffalo in the United States! Today there are only a few herds of bison so you probably won't find one in your neighborhood. But you MIGHT find a buffalo nickel!

You know why? Well, usually only the pictures of important people are used on money. But the buffalo was such an important part of the history of America that a buffalo was once pictured on the American nickel! So someday you MIGHT find a buffalo nickel. And someday, when it's icy cold at your house, you might wish God had given YOU that furry cape instead of giving it to the buffalo!

Of course, you'd have to wear the cape all year long and a furry cape wouldn't feel too good on a hot summer day, would it?

You know you don't NEED a cape to be a crusader. If you try, you might think of a way to help somebody this very day! Maybe somebody might like to get a letter from you or a phone call or a visit. Maybe somebody might wish you would help clear the table or wash the dishes tonight. A buffalo couldn't do that—but YOU could!

Buffalo

A Thief in the Night

Notice how a raccoon looks like he's wearing a mask. No wonder! This cute little animal is a thief! He will swipe food from anywhere he can find it. And he has hands that can even

Raccoon

open latches so he can get in a house and run around, open cabinet doors and go through garbage sacks. Of course, he doesn't KNOW he's a thief. He just knows he's hungry!

There's another funny thing about raccoons. When they're near a stream or any kind of water, they like to dip their food in the water. It looks like they are washing it underwater with their paws but scientists think they just like wet food better than dry food.

Did you ever dip a donut in milk? Maybe the raccoon would like that too. So watch out. If there's a raccoon in your neighborhood, he might sneak up and try to grab your donut!

Pretend you're a raccoon today and think about all the foods you might like to "dip!" How about a carrot stick, a potato chip, a celery stick, a taco chip, a piece of apple or pear? How about dipping a marshmallow into a cup of hot chocolate or a strawberry into melted chocolate? Isn't it great that God gave us so many "dippy" foods— as well as dippy animals!

Long Lashes, Terrible Tempers!

The camel is famous for being able to go for days or even weeks without drinking any water. Do you know why? When a camel comes to a watering hole, he can slurp up 30 gallons of water in 10 minutes. That's almost 500 cups full of water! Could you drink that much water in 10 minutes? Could you drink that much water if you had all day? Probably not!

The camel can store the water in its body for a very long time (most people think he stores it in the hump on his back but that's not true) and can travel across the desert without getting thirsty.

God also gave the camel other things to help him survive in the hot, dry, dusty desert. There's a thick web of skin between his two toes so he won't sink into the sand. And the camel has lots of eyelashes! In fact, he has two or three ROWS of eyelashes to protect his eyes from the wind and sand in a sandstorm. But the camel has one bad thing too—a terrible temper! Camels spit! They complain. And sometimes they get really mad at the camel drivers. But maybe you'd get mad too if you spent all your time traveling across a dusty

desert, carrying 30 gallons of water!

Why don't you get out a mirror today and try to COUNT your eyelashes!

Then have a nice cool drink of water and thank God for water and camels and eyelashes and people and animals who have GOOD tempers!

Camel

35

Who's Been Dragon Around?

Did you ever hear a story about a dragon? You might "meet" a make-believe dragon in a fairy tale, but did you know there is a REAL lizard so big it is known as a dragon? This lizard can grow to be 10 feet long! If one of these "dragons" came into your house, it would fill up your bedroom because it would be as long as most rooms are wide!

This lizard is called the Komodo dragon because most of them live on an Indonesian island called Komodo Island. But recently a few have been hatched at zoos in

Komodo Dragon

America, so some day you may be able to see a real dragon instead of just reading about one in a fairy tale.

Would you LIKE to see a dragon? Or would you be afraid to look at one? Some of the animals God made DO look scary to humans—but maybe humans look scary to the animals! Did you ever think about that?

Which animals do you think are scary? Which animals do you think are friendly? And which animals do you think would be scared of YOU? Pretend you are an animal today and try to imagine how that animal might feel. Would it feel scary—or scared—or friendly? Just remember, friendly animals—and friendly people—have MORE friends.

Kangaroo

The Peekaboo Kangaroo

Kangaroo babies spend a lot of time peek-a-booing out of their mother's pouch. You know why? They live there for six months after they are born! You know why? A just-born kangaroo is only one inch long—about the size of a person's thumb! Such a tiny baby needs a safe cozy spot where she can start to grow. And she sure does grow! Some kangaroos grow to be six feet tall, or as tall as a teen-ager.

The kangaroo mother's pocket-home is lined with fur to keep the baby warm and protected—and it's also a good way to take the baby traveling, since kangaroos don't have strollers or baby carriages. Even after the baby grows and learns to hop and jump, she still travels in her mother's pouch when danger is near because the mother can hop away a lot faster!

A six-month old kangaroo is the size of a puppy and is called a Joey. A grown-up female is a Blue Flier and an adult male is called a Boomer!

Did you know God made 120 different KINDS of kangaroos? But God gave ALL kangaroos strong hind legs so they're all "high jumpers!" Some can jump 40 feet in a single leap! Can YOU jump that far? Probably not.

God gave you the kind of legs that can do LOTS of things—climb up on your grandpa's knee, climb a tree, climb a ladder and climb a mountain! Aren't you glad you can walk, run, and climb instead of having to hop everywhere you go?

Yipes, a White Stripe!

When you see this black furry animal with a white stripe down its back, watch out!

This animal LOOKS so cute and friendly, you might want to pat its head or pet its pretty fur—but instead, you might have to hold your nose and run as fast as you can to get away from its smell. Yep, this is a skunk!

The skunk is not mean. He doesn't "shoot" unless he gets scared by some intruder. Then he turns his back and lifts up his tail as a WARNING. If the intruder doesn't leave fast, the skunk shoots out a really BAAAAAD SMELLING spray. That's why other animals and SMART people do NOT scare a skunk!

The skunk's spray is so bad, if it hits your face, it can make you blind or keep you from breathing—but just for a little while, just long enough for the skunk to escape. And people who get skunk spray on their clothes have to throw away the clothes because the odor will NEVER come out. So if you ever see a little black animal with a WHITE stripe down its back, yell YIPES! and run in the opposite direction.

But if you see a skunk in a zoo, that skunk has been "de-odorized"! Its stinky spray shooter has been removed so it's safe to get close and make friends.

God gave the skunk a BAD smell to protect itself but God

put lots of GOOD smells in the world for YOU to enjoy—flowers in the garden, popcorn popping at the movies, burgers barbecuing in the backyard. What good things can you smell right now? What do you think is the most swell smell?

Skunk

41

Hush, Bush Baby!

When British explorers were in the African "bush"—which is like a forest—they heard a sound like the loud screechy shouts of a very excited child.

They discovered the sound came from this woolly animal. That's why they named it a "bush baby."

God made the bush baby very small but gave her very LARGE eyes. He also made her back legs

Bush Baby

longer than her front legs and gave her a LONG tail to use as a rudder so that when she jumps such long distances, it looks like she's flying through the tree tops.

Did you know when a baby bush baby travels with her mother, she hangs on by wrapping that long tail around her mother's neck? Grown-up bush babies sleep during the day. And sometimes as many as 20 of them will crowd together to sleep in a hollow tree trunk! Then at dusk, they wake up and split up into family groups to go hunting for their favorite foods—fruit, flowers, and honey from wild bees.

Although bush babies like to fly high, when they settle down, African tribes often keep them as pets.

Would you like to have a pet bush baby? Remember—it would make a lot of noise! If you think your dog's barking bothers you neighbors.... Why don't you make a list of ALL the animals you think would make good pets. Then list all the animals you think would NOT be good pets. How MANY animals can you list that God made and put on the earth for you to think about, learn about—and maybe even have as a friend?

Mandrill

A Monkey with a Lipstick Nose

Did you know God "painted" the mandrill's face? He did! The mandrill—the largest of all the monkeys—has a face marked with bright blue and purple stripes and a long, shiny, lipstick-red nose!

Because of its strange colors, the male mandrill LOOKS more ferocious than he is—especially when he bares his long fang-like teeth! But that's just the mandrill's way of showing you he's NOT going to attack!

And guess what! ONLY the daddy mandrills look like they've put lipstick on their noses. The mama mandrills' faces don't have bright red noses. But both the mamas AND the papas have a strange way of walking. They walk on their fingers and toes so that the palms of their hands and the soles of their feet do NOT touch the ground!

Could YOU walk with just the tips of your fingers and toes touching the ground?

Try it today and if anyone asks, tell them you're meandering like a mandrill, making mandrill moves, or doing the "Mandrill March."

OR you could tell them you're just monkeying around!

Bamboo for Breakfast?

Did you know the panda bear eats bamboo for breakfast, lunch, and dinner! And God gave her a "sixth finger" to help her do that! The extra finger is really more like a thumb that grows out of the panda's wrist and helps her hold and strip the OUTSIDE of the bamboo stalk before she eats

Panda Bear

the INSIDE. And the panda NEEDS whatever help she can get because she likes to eat about 600 bamboo stems a day!

God also made the panda's throat with a tough lining to protect her from the sharp splinters of the bamboo. So don't YOU try to eat any bamboo because God made YOUR throat with a softer lining—just right for pizza, ice cream and food that does NOT have splinters in it!

The giant panda bear lives in the misty mountain forests of China and has thick, waterproof fur to keep her warm and dry. But the panda is not the only kind of bear God made. Can you think of other kinds?

No, God did NOT make teddy bears. But God DID make the polar bear, the brown bear, the black bear, the grizzly bear and even a spectacled bear. The spectacled bear has white markings around his eyes and he looks like he's wearing glasses! God must have had a lot of fun making THAT bear!

God made lots of different kinds of bears—just like he made lots of different kinds of people. Don't you think that was a beary good idea?

A Prickly Problem

Ouch! Here's an animal that can run backwards and has a tail full of needles! The sharp, bristly spikes on a porcupine's back are actually called "quills" and they are soft and fur-like when the porcupine is growing up—but gradually they get strong and sharp. A grown-up porcupine can have as many as 30,000 quills on his back and tail and some are five inches long—about as long as a ball-point pen!

When the porcupine thinks he is in danger, he raises up his quills to make himself look bigger and meaner, and then he shakes the quills to make a loud, clattering noise. If this is not enough to scare away an enemy, the porcupine swivels around fast and charges backwards, aiming those needle-like quills so he can spear his opponent—right in the nose!

Some people think the porcupine can shoot the quills at his target but that isn't true. He has to run backward, aim, and spear! Ouch! Imagine getting stuck in the nose with a needle as long as a ball-point pen but even sharper!

Porcupine

That sure was a funny way for God to make a porcupine, wasn't it? But it works! Nobody wants to pick on a porcupine!

Why don't you go out in the yard today and try to run backward (it's a lot harder than running forward!) While you're running, think about the times when YOU might have hurt somebody by aiming mean, sharp words at them—instead of quills. Tell God you're sorry and promise yourself you will try to NEVER act like a porcupine again!

49

The Meerkat Babysitters' Club

This is not a mere cat! It's a meerkat—a small mongoose that lives far away in the dry sandy plains of southern Africa. Meerkats are very different looking and acting than kitty cats. In fact, some of them have jobs as babysitters!

The meerkats like to stick together. A "pack" will usually include from 30 to 50 meerkats who cooperate to "keep house." Each day a "raiding party" goes out looking for food—and while they're gone, the "teenage" girl meerkats babysit and take care of the babies!

Afrikaners call the meerkats "sticktails" because a group will often be seen, standing upright, propped up on their tails. Sometimes they are just sunning themselves. Sometimes they are on lookout duty, watching for enemies who might threaten their home.

When the meerkats see an enemy approaching, they jump up and down together, shouting a shrill battle cry and scuffing up the dust to make a cloud around them so it will look like they are a large pack of frightful fighters. Isn't it

neat the way God made
meerkats so cooperative?
They hunt together,
sun together, jump
together and even
babysit together!

Are YOU like a
meerkat? When you
are in a group, do you
like to help and share
and work together?
Sit or stand in the sun
today and think
about what YOU
could do to be as
cooperative as a
meerkat!

Meerkat

Flying a Ring-Tailed Flag

Take a look at this ring-tailed lemur's tail. It is much longer than the lemur's body! The lemurs usually travel in groups of about 20, and when they travel they wave their tails up high like you might wave a flag.

Wouldn't you like to see a ring-tailed parade? However, you would probably have to go to the island of Madagascar in the Indian Ocean to see it since that's the ONLY place wild lemurs live.

Lemurs and other animals—like the lorises, tarsiers, monkeys and apes—are primates. And so are YOU! Did you know God made you a primate? If you don't believe that, here's a checklist you can use to see if you can do what other primates do.

Can you grip a branch with your thumb opposite your fingers? Do your claws (or hands) have nails on the end of the "fingers"? Can you turn the palm of your hand up to put food into your mouth? Are your eyes on the FRONT of your head instead of on the side—so you have stereoscopic vision? If you answered yes, yes, yes, and yes—then you must be a primate!

Do you know why having eyes on the front of your head is important at meal time? Close one eye and try to eat something. You might end up with an apple in your eye or a spoon up your nose! Aren't you glad God made you a primate—even if he didn't give you a ring-tailed flag to fly!

Lemur

How Slow Is a Sloth?

Here's an animal that spends most of its life hanging UPSIDE DOWN from a tree branch—even when it's asleep! And the sloth sleeps a lot. When he is not sleeping, the sloth moves VERRRY slowly. So how slow is a sloth? Well, when you are in a car on the highway, going 60 miles per hour, you move a mile a MINUTE. If a sloth did travel a mile, it would take him an HOUR!

A sloth eats leaves, buds and twigs from the tree where he lives and seldom climbs down to the ground. Since he is usually upside down, God made the sloth's fur grow thick on his stomach and thin on his back, unlike the way fur grows on most other animals like dogs—thick on the back and thin on the stomach. This makes it possible for water to drain off the sloth's fur when it rains—because the sloth is NEVER going to move fast enough to get in out of the rain!

And guess what! During the rainy season, the sloth turns green! Why? Because little plants called algae grow all over his gray fur—like they might grow over a log or a rock that doesn't move!

Sloth

Do YOU ever move as slow as a sloth—like maybe when it's time to do a chore around the house or when it's time to go to bed at night? The sloth is happy moving slowly because he has nowhere to go. But YOU have things to do and places to go—so don't just hang around like a sloth today. Read a book, run a race, draw a picture or surprise your folks by doing a chore or getting to bed REALLY FAST! And be grateful that you don't have to sleep hanging upside down in a tree!

You Otter See This Sea Otter!

Let's play! Full of fun and frolic, the sea otter romps about the river bank or seashore just like you might have fun at a swimming pool. An otter loves to play! But then she settles down to wash her face and comb her coat with a careful paw. The sea otter depends on a squeaky-clean fur to keep

Sea Otter

her warm in cold waters (instead of a fat layer under the skin like some animals have) so it's important to her to be well-groomed!

The sea otter knows how to use "tools" too—which is very unusual for an animal. She sometimes uses seaweed to "tie" her family together to keep them from floating away in a strong current. And when it's dinner time, instead of sitting at a table with a napkin in her lap, the otter floats on her back in the water with a rock on her tummy! Then she takes some clams she has caught, holds them in her paws, and hits them against the rock to crack the shells. Finally, she is able to feast on a clam dinner!

God gave this furry little creature a playful nature—but also a careful one. She knows when it's time to stop playing and time to get to work or get cleaned up. Do YOU know when it's time to stop playing and wash your face and hands to get ready to eat a clam dinner? Maybe you'd rather have a hamburger or a hot dog for dinner—but aren't you glad you can eat it sitting at a table with a napkin on your lap instead of floating on your back with a rock on your tummy?

A Howling Good Time

Did you ever hear a wolf howl? Did you know that when a pack of wolves start howling together, each one chooses a different note so no two howls sound exactly alike? They sound like they're trying to form a rock group so they can record an album—or maybe they'd just like to sing in the church choir!

Wolf

When the wolf is not "singing," he is a wild and canny animal. God gave the golden-eyed wolf a regal, proud look—but also a playful nature. Since the wolf is related to the dog, he sometimes likes to romp and play in the snow, and gets his packmates' attention by nose-bumping, rough-housing and pretend biting—just like some dogs do.

Do YOU like to sing—or howl? Go somewhere today where no one will hear you and try to howl like a wolf. Then think about your voice. Aren't you glad that God gave you a voice that can do MORE than howl? Your voice can also sing and talk and tell other people what you think, what you want, what you dream about being some day—or maybe how much you love them.

Talk to someone today. Whisper a secret to someone. Call someone on the phone. Try to yodel. Sing a loud song. Sing a soft song. And then talk to God with a prayer and tell him thanks for giving you the amazing gift of a voice!

Oh Deer! Is It Rein-ing? And Is He Wearing Snow Shoes?

You know all about Santa and his reindeer, don't you? But did you know that another name for a reindeer is "caribou"? And did you know Eskimos like to drink reindeer milk? And did you know God gave the reindeer snowshoe feet? It's true. The reindeer has broad hooves on his feet to make it easier for him to walk in deep snow. And that's important because—as you know—a reindeer lives where the snow is really deep!

The reindeer also uses his hooves as a snow-scraper! Did you ever watch someone use a scraper to get the snow off a car windshield? The reindeer uses a hoof to scrape the snow away from the ground so he can nibble the nice green moss that grows deep beneath the snow.

Reindeer

60

And did you know that lots of reindeer take a trip twice a year? They do! The whole pack packs up and travels 600 miles, following trails that their families have used for hundreds of years. They have TWO places they like to live. Half the year they live on the "tundra" which is a treeless plain and the other half of the year, they live in forests where Christmas trees grow! (Probably that's the half-year when they help Santa!)

Do YOU like to travel? Have you ever walked in snowshoes? Have you ever had a glass of reindeer milk? Drink a glass of regular milk today and tell God thanks for milk and snowshoes and Christmas trees and tundras and caribou—and all the people who love YOU!

The Puzzling Platypus

This animal is not a duck but it has a bill like a duck—and webbed feet too. It's not a beaver but it has a tail like a beaver. It's not a fish but it spends a lot of time in the water. It's not a bird or a chicken but it lays eggs. This is one of the strangest animals God ever made—the duck-billed platypus!

When someone first told Europeans about this Australian animal, they thought it was a joke—and no wonder! This animal DOES sound pretty funny, doesn't it? But it is a REAL animal.

Although the platypus has a bill and feet like a duck, she is not covered with feathers but with soft fur. And although she LOOKS like she has no ears, she can hear very well because she has ears inside her head! And the platypus has a deep fold of skin that comes down and covers her eyes when she swims—so she doesn't need swim-goggles like you might use!

Wouldn't you like to SEE a duck-billed platypus in person? Wouldn't you like to have a camera and take a picture of one to show your friends? You might not get that chance since the platypus is VERY rare—but you COULD take photos—or draw pictures—of the animals in your neighborhood!

Why don't you start today to look around and see how many animals live near you. Then make a scrapbook with photos or drawings of all of them. You won't find any animals as strange as a platypus—but it would be fun to show your friends your own hand-made Neighborhood Animal Book!

Platypus

The Reckless Red Fox–And the Refrigerator!

When someone is clever or cunning, they are often described as being "sly as a fox" or "smart as a fox." Foxes DO seem to be smart—but they are reckless too! The red fox is often sly enough to outsmart

Red Fox

hunters who try to trap him or hound dogs who try to track him. The red fox can dig up and set off a trap without getting caught or double back on his own tracks so the dogs get confused and lose his scent. That is pretty smart BUT the red fox will sometimes pass up a safe hiding place and keep running when he's being chased—as though he enjoys the game! And that's pretty reckless.

The red fox is just one of the foxes God made. God also made the gray fox who can climb trees and the white Arctic fox who uses a refrigerator for her food! In the Arctic summer, this fox will hide eggs and other kinds of food under rocks. Since it is VERY cold in the Arctic even in the summer, the food keeps fresh just like it would in a refrigerator. When winter comes and fresh food is even more scarce than usual, the Arctic fox goes to her refrigerator and helps herself to a snack.

Today, when you go to the refrigerator for a snack, think about the foxes. While you're enjoying your snack, imagine that you are a fox. Imagine watching out for the hunter's traps or being chased by hound dogs or looking for food to put into your refrigerator. What kind of fox would you be— smart or reckless? Which kind of PERSON is it be BETTER to be—smart or reckless?

Black and White or White and Black

Do you think the zebra is white with black stripes or black with white stripes? Whichever way she is, the zebra is a wild horse which God painted with stripes to give her PROTECTION!

Zebras may all LOOK alike but did you know each zebra has its OWN pattern of stripes? The white stripes look like LIGHT and the black stripes are like SHADOW and this makes the zebra hard to spot in tall grass.

When the zebras are in a group, they face in different directions to make a zig-zag sight. When they run from an enemy, they scatter and RUN in different directions so the sight of zebra stripes zig-zagging makes a blur and CONFUSES the enemy! And this helps the zebra escape.

The zebra's striped protection gave some people a good idea in World War II. They painted merchant ships with zebra stripes— and this made it hard for submarines to find them as a target!

Zebra

Aren't you surprised that a zebra and a merchant ship would have something alike? What do YOU have that's like a zebra? Do you ever wear striped clothes? Can you run fast? Do you ever like to "camouflage" yourself the way the zebra does in the tall grasses (like maybe when you dress up for Halloween?)

Each creature on earth is different—yet they all have some things that are similar. They all need food and water. They are all afraid of enemies. And they were all made by God. Aren't you glad you're one of them!

Animal Appendix

What ELSE would you like to know about the animals God made? Did you know giraffes can't swim, elephants can't jump, and kangaroos can't walk backwards? Aren't you glad YOU can do ALL those things? Here are some more questions and answers about animals.

Do Animals Talk?

Animals don't talk the same way YOU do but they certainly do "speak" with other animals. There are different ways humans to talk to each other—with words, sign language, body language (like when you frown or smile or pout or cross your arms across your chest)—and there are different ways animals talk too.

Birds chirp, whistle, and make beautiful musical sounds and songs. Cats purr and meow, dogs bark and whine, chickens cackle and crow. Wolves howl, lions roar, chimps chatter. And whales whistle.

Did you know:

◆ Most animals can only make a few different sounds to get a message across. But humans have as many as 40,000 words they can use to let others know they're glad, sad, mad—or hungry!

◆ The sounds of the humpback whale travel through channels in the ocean floor 2,000-4,000 feet under the water's surface, and are carried thousands of miles from one side of the Pacific Ocean to the other!

◆ Some scientists think they've found the BEST example of true animal language. And you won't believe what it is! It isn't the meow or the moo, the chirp or the cock-a-doodle-doo! It isn't even a sound. It's the DANCE of the honeybees! Bees do buzz, but when they want to tell their friends where to find food—and that's VERY important!—they tell them with a DANCE!

Do YOU know how to "talk like the animals?" Try it today. Can you sound like a dog, a cat, a rooster, a cow or a whale? Can you dance like a bee? Maybe you can't. But you CAN speak to your best friend and talk about which animal is your favorite and why. Then maybe you could start to make a list and count how many WORDS you know which you can use to talk and "communicate" with people—and with pets!

Do Animals Smell?

Well, yes, some animals smell BAD—like a wet dog who has been rolling in the mud or a skunk who is mad. But there's a different kind of animal smell. Animals use their sense of smell to "identify" each other and to mark off territory. Each animal seems to have a special odor which it leaves wherever it goes. When other animals sniff around, they can tell which animal lives in what yard or which animal has been taking a walk along your street. They even sniff YOU to see if you have been near some OTHER animal—like a friend's dog or cat.

Why don't YOU become a scent detective and use your sense of smell today to see how many "people" odors you can find in your house? Hint: check out the spices in the kitchen cabinet, the food in the refrigerator, the perfume or after-shave in the bedroom, plants or flowers in bloom—or maybe somebody's dirty socks under the bed! How many scents can you sense?

Are Animals Physically Fit?

Think about the animals you have read about in this book and decide which ones have physical skills.

◆ Which animals are good at running or jumping? Which animals are good "swingers" or acrobats. Can YOU run, jump, swing or walk on a balance beam? Try to do some of those things today.

◆ Which animals would be good at playing the games YOU play? Would a kangaroo be good at jumping rope? Would a kitty cat be good at playing hide-and-seek? Think of all the games you like to play and decide which animals you think would be good at playing those games with you! Who do you think would win the game?

There are SO MANY things to learn and think about the animals God made. After you've read this book, you may want to go to the library and find MORE books about animals. OR you may want to draw a picture of an animal or write a story about an animal. OR you may want to make up a prayer to thank God for all the animals and to say how happy you are to learn about this zany zoo!